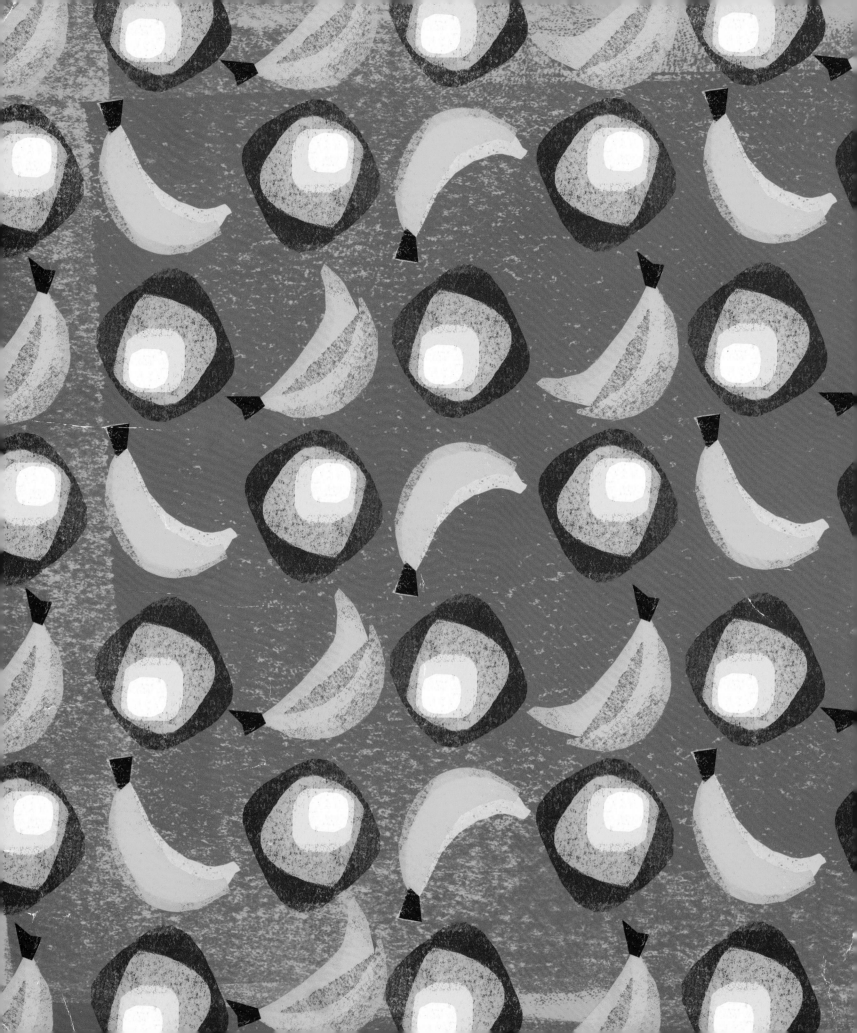

To groovy mover Margot Good! – GPJ

For sister Grace, love LS x

Farshore

First published in Great Britain 2021 by Farshore

An imprint of HarperCollins*Publishers*
1 London Bridge Street, London SE1 9GF
www.farshore.co.uk

HarperCollins*Publishers*
1st Floor, Watermarque Building, Ringsend Road
Dublin 4, Ireland

Text copyright © Gareth P. Jones 2021
Illustrations copyright © Loretta Schauer 2021
Gareth P. Jones and Loretta Schauer have asserted their moral rights.

ISBN 978 1 4052 9884 1
Printed in the UK by Pureprint a CarbonNeutral® company
1

A CIP catalogue record for this title is available from the British Library.

Stay safe online. Farshore is not responsible for content hosted by third parties.

MIX
Paper from
responsible sources
FSC™ C007454

FSC
www.fsc.org

This book is produced from independently certified FSC™ paper
to ensure responsible forest management.

For more information visit: www.harpercollins.co.uk/green

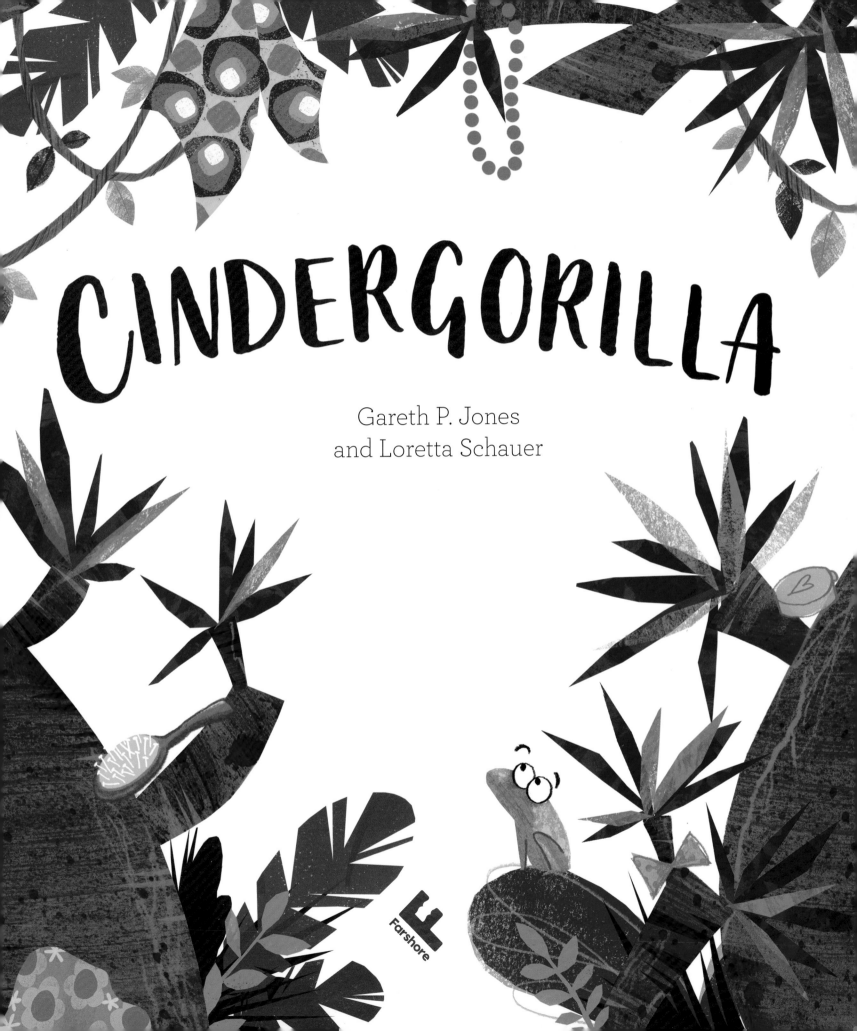

CINDERGORILLA

Gareth P. Jones
and Loretta Schauer

Once up on Hairy Tail Mountain, in a deep green jungle by a gushing waterfall, lived Cindergorilla.

Cinder lived with her Aunt Linda and two cousins, Gertrude and Grace, who spent their days being mean to her and ordering her about.

"Those banana skins won't pick up themselves," said Gertrude.

"Come and do my hair," Grace demanded.

"And don't forget to wash the dishes!" said Aunt Linda.

Cinder would have been very unhappy, except for one thing . . .

She LOVED to dance!
She boogied with her broom
and moonwalked with her mop.

She twirled as she tidied and wiggled as she washed up.

Cinder longed to go to the Disco Ball, but her aunt always said no!

One Saturday, Cinder's cousins were getting ready for a big night out when Grace announced: **"Travis the Disco Prince is looking for a new dance partner!"**

TRAVIS

PRINCE of the DISCO

"I'm the best dancer," boasted Gertrude.

"But Travis will want someone with style," argued Grace.

"I'm not sure I'd want a dance partner," said Cinder, "but I would love to go to the Disco Ball."

"You! Dance?" sniffed Gertude.

"Don't make us laugh!" snorted Grace.

"Yes, tidying up bananas is more your thing," added her aunt.

And off they went, leaving Cinder with a list of jobs to do.

Cinder was dancing a sad, slow dance with her broom when suddenly, with a **FLASH!** and a **BANG!** and a

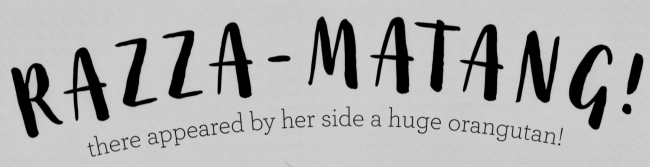

RAZZA-MATANG!

there appeared by her side a huge orangutan!

"Who are you?"
asked Cinder.

"I'm your Hairy Godmother.
I've come to make things right.
Cindergorilla, you *shall* dance
at the Disco Ball tonight!"

She flicked her wand and . . .

Cinder was transformed into a sparkling disco diva!

"To make your magical makeover complete,
put these banana skins onto your feet."

"Won't they be
a bit slippery?"
asked Cinder.

With another flick of the Hairy Godmother's wand,
the banana skins became a groovy pair of dancing shoes.

"Wow!" exclaimed Cinder.
"Thanks, Hairy Godmother!"

Her Hairy Godmother smiled, then said:

"Be warned, sweet Cinder,
my magic will fade.
Be home before sunrise.
Don't get waylaid."

And with that, Cinder went off to the ball.

Cinder felt nervous as she stepped onto the dance floor.
But she soon lost herself in the music
and made lots of new friends!

She grooved with
some gibbons.

She breakdanced with a baboon.

She was in the middle
of a dance-off with
a chimpanzee . . .

... when another gorilla barged his way over and said: "Wow! You can really move. You're almost as good as me!"

"Who are you?" asked Cinder.

"You don't know?" he laughed. "I'm Travis, the Disco Prince. From now on, you can dance with ME!"

Just then, a beam of morning sunlight hit the disco ball and Cinder remembered the Hairy Godmother's warning.

"I have to go!" she gasped.

"GO?" said Travis. "But you haven't seen my best move yet!"

Cinder turned and fled, but the magic was fading fast and a shoe slipped off her foot.

"This shoe belongs to the second greatest dancer at the disco!" cried Travis, picking it up. "I shall not rest until I find its owner."

But shoes aren't always the best way of finding someone . . .

"No!"

"Nope!"

"Definitely not!"

Travis was almost ready to give up. But there was one more place to try.

Gertrude and Grace squealed as Travis burst in holding the shoe.

"Behold!" he said. "This shoe belongs to –"

"It looks like one of mine!" interrupted Grace.

"It's bound to fit my dainty feet," said Gertrude.

But the shoe didn't
fit Gertrude,

or Grace.

Then Travis spotted Cinder. **"Hey, don't I recognise you?"** he said.
He grabbed the shoe and shoved it onto Cinder's foot . . .

"It's the perfect fit
so let's dance every night!
As the star I will lead,
but I'll share my limelight."

"Cinder's the mystery
dancer?" screeched
Gertrude and Grace.

"Thank you, Travis," said Cinder, "but I don't really want
a dance partner. I just want to dance with my new friends!"

"And so you shall!" said a familiar voice . . .

With a **FLASH!** and a **BANG!** and a

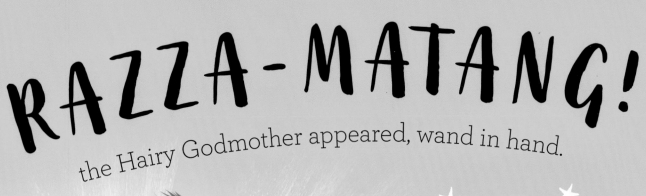

RAZZA-MATANG!

the Hairy Godmother appeared, wand in hand.

"Just a little wave here and a little wave there,
and the single shoe will become a pair."

"No, no, no!" cried Cinder's aunt.
"She can't go to the Disco Ball.
She has to tidy up this place."

The Hairy Godmother said:

"Gertrude, Grace, and you, Aunt Linda,
in future you'll all be much kinder to Cinder.
The lesson to learn is one you can guess –
tidy your things and clean up YOUR mess!"

So, Cinder's aunt and cousins helped
tidy up. Even Travis mucked in.

Then the Hairy Godmother gave her wand one final shake.

Suddenly the whole place was filled with music and lights and disco dancers!

And the Hairy Godmother sang:

"With these last words, this story ends.
Put on your shoes and dance with your friends.
Get down to the sound of music and laughter,
Cinder will dance . . .

groovily ever after!"

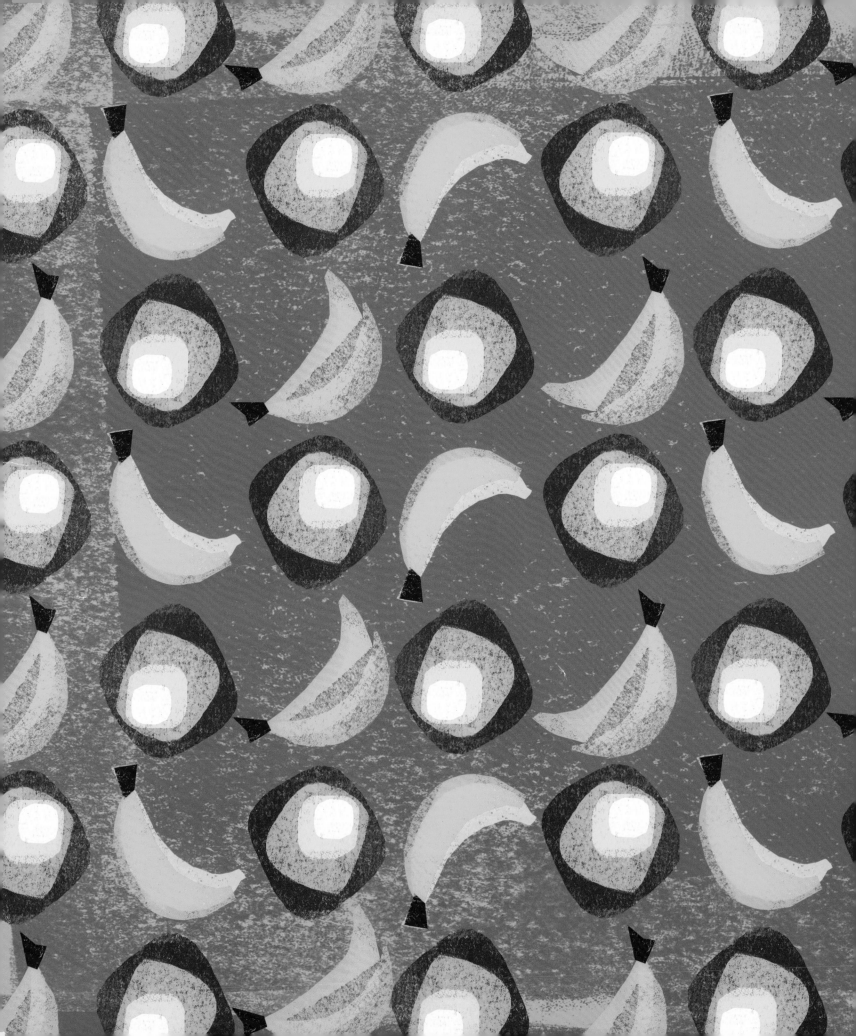

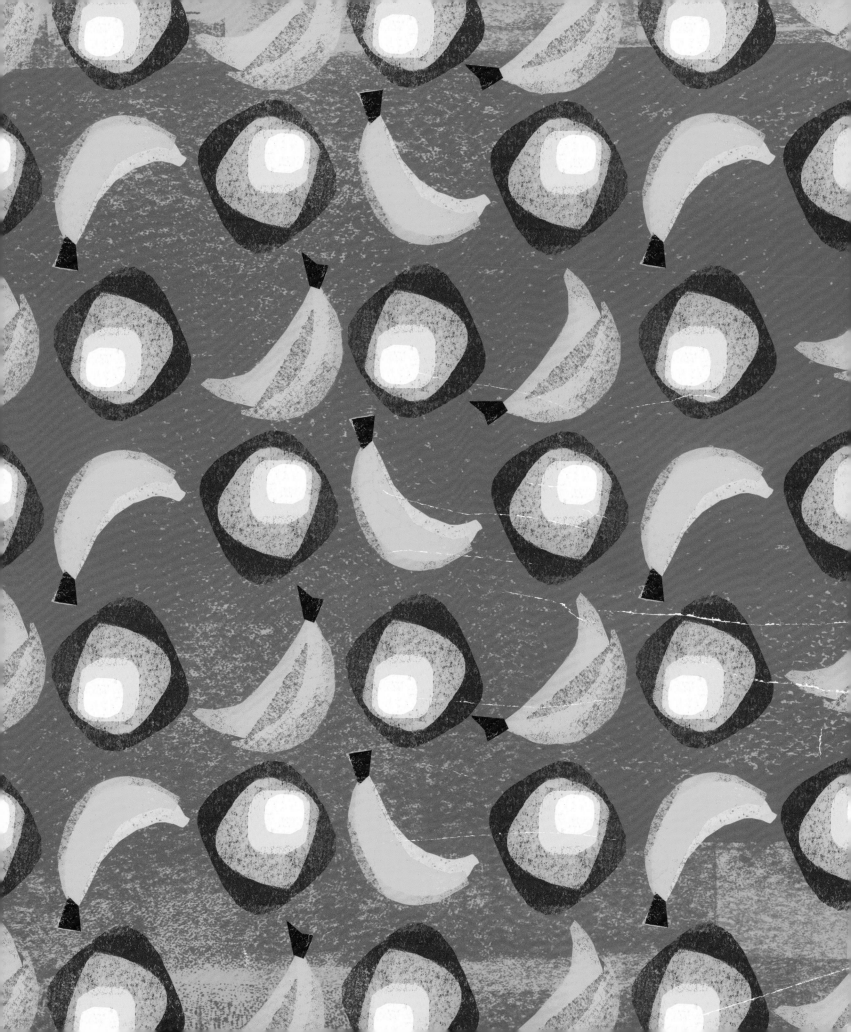